This book belongs to
_____
_____
_____
_____

For Alex —
 Who loves ponies & Dallys as much as I do
With Best Wishes —
 Jay Claxton

Also by Joy Claxton in conjunction with Richard and Vivian Ellis

Donkey Driving
Make the most of Carriage Driving

published by J.A.Allen

ACKNOWLEDGEMENTS

I would like to give many thanks to Carol Gillings for her friendship and for guiding me through the many pitfalls of my inadequate useage of English grammar. Also for her great patience with both me and her computer which has a mind of its own.

Thanks also to my friends who encouraged me to produce this book, mostly I suspect because they wanted to read it with their children and grandchildren.

Produced and edited by Carol Gillings
Carol@cgillings.fslife.co.uk

Order this book online at www.trafford.com/07-0587
or email orders@trafford.com

Most Trafford titles are also available at major online book retailers.

© Copyright 2007 Joy Claxton

All rights reserved. No part of this publication may be reproduced, stored in a retrieval system, or transmitted, in any form or by any means, electronic, mechanical, photocopying, recording, or otherwise, without the written prior permission of the author.

Note for Librarians: A cataloguing record for this book is available from Library and Archives Canada at www.collectionscanada.ca/amicus/index-e.html

Printed in Victoria, BC, Canada.

ISBN: 978-1-4251-2185-3

We at Trafford believe that it is the responsibility of us all, as both individuals and corporations, to make choices that are environmentally and socially sound. You, in turn, are supporting this responsible conduct each time you purchase a Trafford book, or make use of our publishing services. To find out how you are helping, please visit www.trafford.com/responsiblepublishing.html

Our mission is to efficiently provide the world's finest, most comprehensive book publishing service, enabling every author to experience success. To find out how to publish your book, your way, and have it available worldwide, visit us online at www.trafford.com/10510

Trafford PUBLISHING

www.trafford.com

North America & international
toll-free: 1 888 232 4444 (USA & Canada)
phone: 250 383 6864 ♦ fax: 250 383 6804
email: info@trafford.com

The United Kingdom & Europe
phone: +44 (0)1865 722 113 ♦ local rate: 0845 230 9601
facsimile: +44 (0)1865 722 868 ♦ email: info.uk@trafford.com

10 9 8 7 6 5 4 3 2 1

Tales told to Greta

Written and Illustrated
by
Joy Claxton

FOREWORD

I owned a cob who was rather lonely in her field, so I bought a donkey to be her companion. My sister's children chose to name this donkey Daisy. They enjoyed riding her, and doing all the grooming and mucking out that went with being responsible little donkey owners. They loved her very much.

However, my job with carriage horses meant leaving home and taking my animals with me. They lived at a do-it-yourself livery yard near Dunstable. Whilst there, Daisy gave birth and Daniel and Nina came to see their new foal and, logically, they named her Marguerite – a variety of cultivated daisy!

Whilst on this visit they met all the other animals at the yard, asking many questions about them. During our long drive back to their home near Dartford I kept them entertained with stories about the horses and ponies they had met, and of the old coaching roads along which we were driving.

Having done a few sketches of the donkey foal it occured to me that here was the basis for a book.

However, time passes – Daisy died and a companion donkey was found for Greta. He was white, and a white masculine floral name was sought – logic had it once again – Cauli-flower!

Over the seasons we all had lots of fun together riding and driving the donkeys, until I found that the children had grown up and I was left driving a tandem of donkeys by myself.

Now there are grand-nieces and -nephews who come to visit Greta and Cauli and it is to them and their parents that I dedicate this book.

Joy Claxton

CONTENTS

Greta is born	1
Shah – the Arab's Tale	4
Hamish – the Shetland Pony's Tale	8
Truett – the Dalmatian's Tale	13
Prince – the Shire Horse's Tale	17
The Story of Balaam	23
High Tree Lady – the Thoroughbred's Tale	26
Raven – the Fell Pony's Tale	31
York – the Cleveland Bay's Tale	36
Megan – the Welsh Pony's Tale	42
A Winter Tale	52
Useful addresses	62

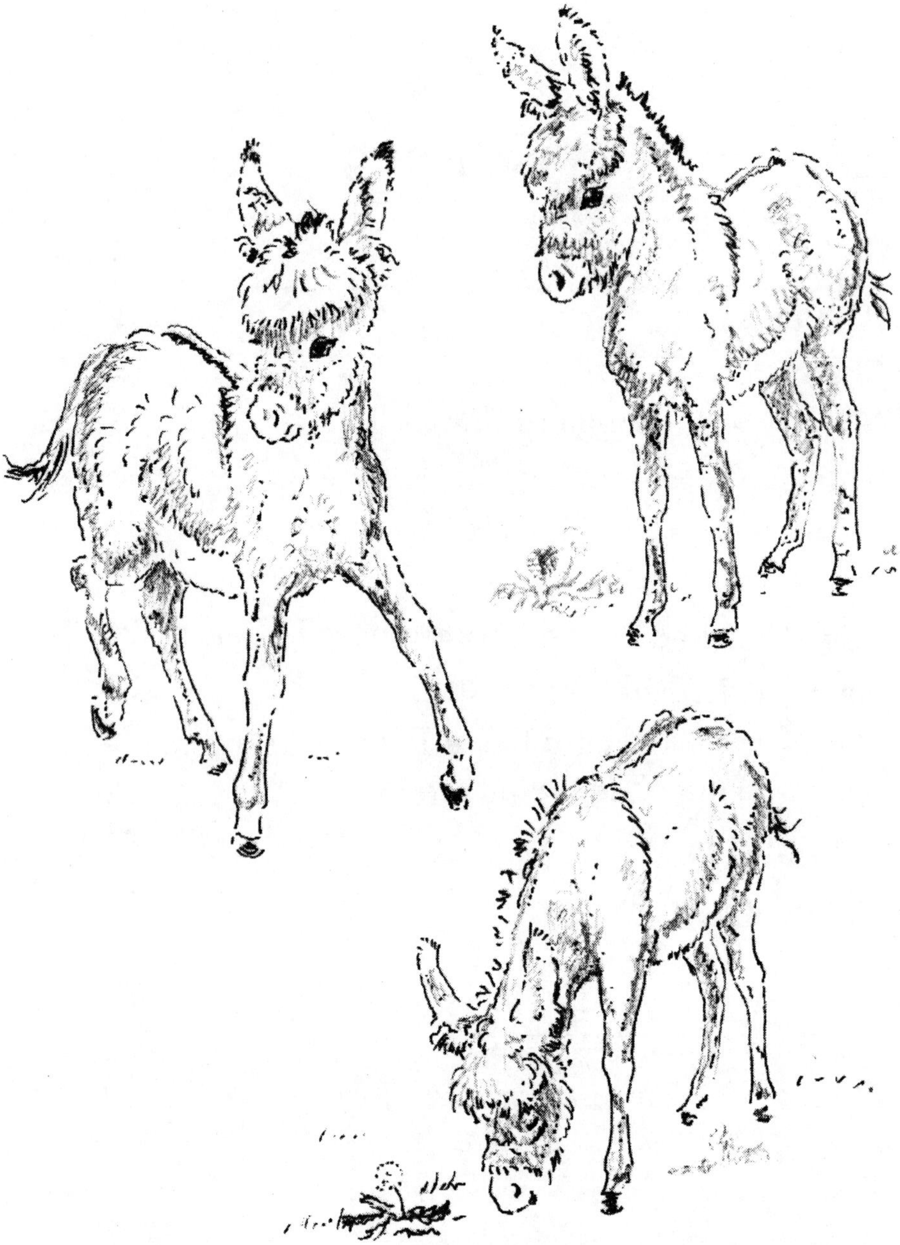

GRETA IS BORN

Early on a June morning, while the sun spread its gentle warmth over the field, Marguerite was born. She lay resting in the grass among the buttercups and the sweetly-scented white clover flowers, her damp coat drying in the sunshine.

Her mother, whose name was Daisy, gazed proudly at her. She nuzzled Greta, softly pushing at her to wake up and try to stand and take her first drink of milk. After several tries, frequently toppling over sideways and onto her nose, she learned to manage her long legs and to balance well enough to suckle from her mother.

As the sunshine grew hot they made their way to the shade of a great tree. Here it was cool, and the sunlight danced in little golden puddles on the ground, as the breeze played through the leaves. Beside the tree was a fence, and on the other side stood a group of horses and ponies sleepily swishing their long tails to keep the flies away. One pony came to take a look at Greta and welcome her, but she was a little shy at first and pressed close to her mother's side.

The children who sometimes rode Daisy came to visit. They brought carrots to feed to Daisy and she crunched them up with her strong teeth, but Greta who only had tiny nipper teeth could not eat them, so she had lots of extra pats and cuddles instead which she really enjoyed.

The children were accompanied by their Dalmatian dog who ran around the fieldlooking for rabbits to chase, but they had all hurried off safely to their homes on the other side of the fence, so the dog just ran – because he liked to. He knew that he must be gentle when he came near to the donkeys so that he did not frighten them, and was content just to stay quietly with them.

As the long summer days passed Greta grew strong and inquisitive. She no longer kept so close to Daisy's side, but would wander off and graze among the horses and ponies that shared the field with them. She noticed that they were different from Daisy and her. They had shorter ears and their voices were higher-pitched than the donkeys' deep 'eeyore'. They had long manes, not like hers which stood straight up in tufts along her neck, and they had long hair on their tails. Some had lots of hair growing on their legs and some had hardly any. Some were a little taller than she was and some were a lot, lot bigger.

Some days their owners would come and take them away from the field for a while, and later they would return.

Greta asked her mother about all these things. Why? Why? Why? Until, like most mothers, Daisy became tired of answering her.
'Go and ask them yourself' she said 'but be polite.'

3

Shah – the Arab's Tale

Greta looked round the field and saw a handsome figure standing alone – gazing into the far distance – the sun shining on his bright chestnut coat making it glint like fire. She just knew that he would love to talk about himself, so she trotted across the field and greeted him, she had missed him as he had not been in the field for the last few days.

He told her that he was content to relax at home today after his long ride yesterday, when he had carried his rider over hills and moorland, competing against other horses in a long distance endurance ride. This ride had only been thirty miles long, but he and his rider were getting fit for longer rides later in the summer. Greta thought this a fearful long way; when she galloped three times round the field she was quite puffed out and ready for a snooze. Shah snorted at her. 'You are not bred for travelling such long distances as I am' he said, 'my ancestors came from the hot sands of Arabia where we were highly prized. We lived in the same tents as our Bedouin owners. In the Holy Koran it says that no evil spirit will deign to enter the tent where there is a true-bred horse.'

Shah could see that the little donkey was impressed, so he told Greta about Mohammed – blessings be upon him – and how he, himself, had chosen the mares that would found the Arab breed of horses.

He had done this by confining a herd of mares for several days with no water so that they were very thirsty, then He freed them to go and drink, but had then called them back. The faithful ones that returned at once, before they had drunk, were his chosen ones.

'Even now we Arabs have the greatest stamina of any breed, and it is a fact that three of my fleet-footed ancestors were brought to England and all English thoroughbreds can trace their lines back to one of those great stallions. We are the most beautiful breed of horse as well as the most ancient. There are pictures of horses that look just as I do in the rock carvings found in Syria, and in the famous friezes in the Parthenon.'

'It is written in the Holy Koran that, after God had created the horse, He spoke to the magnificent creature saying –

"I have made thee unlike any other
The treasures of this earth lie between thine eyes
Thou shalt cast mine enemies beneath thine hooves,
but thou shalt carry my friends on thy back
This shall be the seat from which praises rise unto Me
Thou shalt find happiness all over the earth
And thou shalt be favoured above all other creatures

For to thee shall accrue the love of the Master of the earth
Thou shalt fly without wings and conquer without sword"'

Having told her this he snorted again and tossed up his head, curled his tail high and trotted off with long, floating strides that took him quickly to the far side of the great field.

Greta watched him in amazement, and then gave her own little snort and imitated his trot back to where her mother was quietly grazing.

HAMISH – THE SHETLAND PONY'S TALE

One morning Greta found herself grazing near an untidy white pony called Hamish, who came and stood beside her and started to nibble and rub the furry coat on her shoulder. Hamish was about the same height as Greta and it seemed polite to do the same rubbing and scratching back, Greta had to keep spitting out white hairs.

After a while Hamish stopped nibbling her and returned to grazing so the little donkey, wanting to keep his attention, complimented him on being white.

'Actually I am grey' he replied indignantly.
'Oh, but you look so lovely and white' she said.
'All white horses are grey, even if they are white. We have dark skins and when we are born we are black and get paler as we grow older. Actually I am a bit special, most Shetland ponies are black, brown or chestnut, and some are odd colours. They are known as piebald when they have patches of black and white, and skewbald when they are brown and white.'

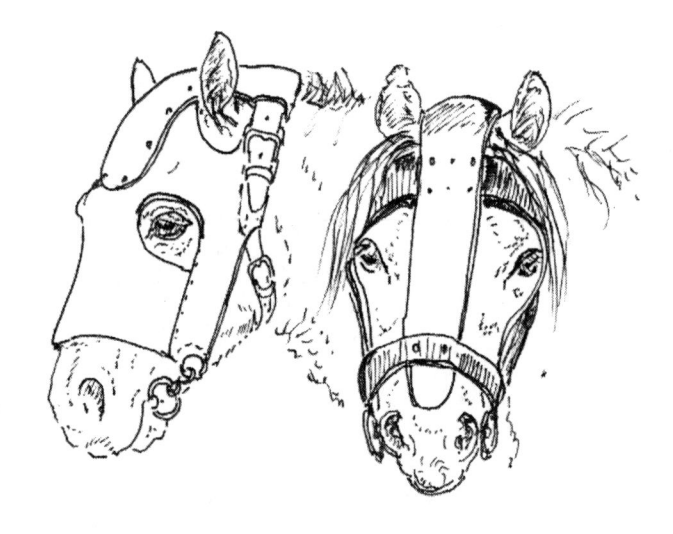

Greta gazed at him in disbelief and wondered if he was teasing her. Hamish went on, 'I came from the Isles of Shetland, which are in the wild seas north of Scotland. We are a small, very hardy breed descended from Celtic ponies. We can live where the grass doesn't grow very well and sometimes we eat seaweed on the beach. To protect us from the cold and wet we grow magnificent thick double winter coats and long manes and tails. We are extremely strong for our size and help on the farms on the Shetland Isles. Many of us were taken and put to work under ground in the coalmines. That was hard, hot work in the dark, and the roads to the coalface were poorly lit. We pulled the tubs of coal to the gathering-points from where it was taken up to the surface. We wore leather helmets attached to our bridles to protect our heads and eyes from falling rocks, and our stables were underground. Once a year, if we were lucky, we were brought to the surface for a holiday in the fields where we could enjoy the sun on our backs, but the bright daylight hurt our eyes after such a long time spent in the darkness of the mines. Most of us were kindly treated and the miners loved us very much, but it is a good thing that those days are gone.'

We modern Shetlands use our strength very differently today. Some of us race at shows and help to raise lots of money for charities which help sick children. Others of us

carry children on our backs, many of them are handicapped or disabled. Our broad, soft backs help them to stretch their limbs, and our gentle movements help them to regain their balance, and all the while they are having fun. Our strong legs can carry them when theirs often will not. Sometimes they will talk to us when they cannot bring themselves to speak to other children and grown-ups. Riding makes these children happy and confident. Myself – I go every week to help except for when I am busy in the theatre.'

Seeing that Greta was interested in all he had to say, he went on to tell her that during the winter months he and three of his friends appeared on stage, taking Cinderella to the ball.

He said, 'we stand quietly with our carriage in the dark at the back of the stage behind a net curtain which has a painting of a huge pumpkin and some mice on it. When Cinderella's Fairy Godmother waves her magic wand the lights at the back of the stage go on and, like magic, the audience can see us and our crystal coach. The net curtain is lifted up and we drive forward to Cinderella who mounts up into her sparkling coach. We shake our heads and make the harness bells ring. Then we drive her away and the audience clap and cheer us. We all feel so proud.'

Greta thought that it all sounded so wonderful. How she wished that she too could act in a play and have all the children laughing and smiling with joy.

'One day you will', promised her mother 'just you wait and see.'

TRUETT – THE DALMATIAN'S TALE

Greta picked carefully at a thistle then crunched it up, gazing into nowhere in particular. Suddenly a rabbit scuttled past her, followed closely by the Dalmatian dog that came with the children when they visited her and Daisy. She watched while the dog ran along by the hedge, stopping now and then to sniff down a hole or look behind a hummock of grass, but the rabbit had gone safely through the hedge and out into the field beyond. The dog came trotting back. 'You didn't run fast enough' said Greta. 'Oh I could have caught up with it if I had tried' he said, 'but if I had, it wouldn't have been there for me to enjoy chasing again tomorrow.'

Greta wondered if he were telling the truth, but was too polite to say so. Instead, she admired his smart white coat with its big dark spots and asked why he had them.

' You see in the olden days we Dalmatians ran with our owner's carriages. We have wonderful shoulders and firm round feet and can trot all day at the same speed as the horses. We trotted along with the carriage and when anyone approached uninvited out we ran and saw them off.'

'I don't see what spots have to do with that' commented the little donkey.

'In the daytime we could be clearly seen and looked very smart beside the carriage, but in the dark it was very different. The spots break up our shape so that we become invisible. Often we would lie down under the carriage at night, guarding it whilst it was standing in the yard at an inn. As you see we have dark noses and eyes which make us look rather like skulls coming from nowhere, so thieves are frightened off before we ever need to bite them.' Greta stepped back quickly in alarm.

'Don't worry I wouldn't harm you. Nowadays we Dallies are family dogs, we still love to travel with our owners, but mostly in their cars. Only a very few of us have the chance to accompany them while they ride their horses and even fewer of us actually run with a carriage. I have the privilege of being able to do so, no doubt you will see me on duty guarding either my master's carriage, or perhaps my other carriage with the baby. I am very fond of my children, and they love me too, although they do complain that my white hairs get all over their clothes.'

With this, he shook himself and loose hairs flew out in a cloud, and the bell which was fixed to his collar rang.

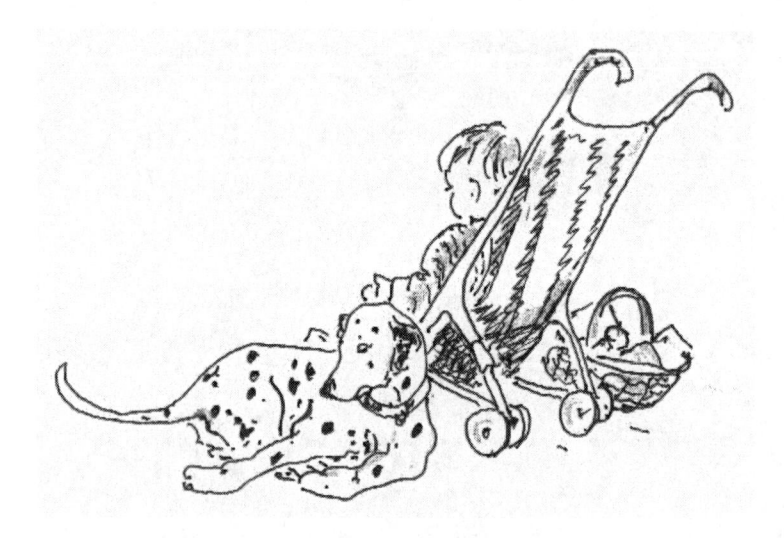

'The bell? We working Dallies all have bells, and when we are trotting along under the carriage our owners can hear where we are and know that we are on duty and haven't gone off rabbiting.' Then he added, with a charming smile and twinkle in his eye – 'and it gives the stable cat a better chance to get away when I chase her in fun'.

PRINCE – THE SHIRE HORSE'S TALE

One hot afternoon Greta was lying near the hedge having a nap. She had become drowsy listening to the droning of the bees who were busy gathering pollen in the sweet-smelling honeysuckle that grew in profusion there. She awoke with a start, feeling the ground tremble.

'I am sorry to have startled you,' said a voice from high above her head. She looked up into a great shadow and found that it was Prince the Shire horse.

'That's all right' she said in a forgiving way as she anxiously looked at the size of Prince's huge feet that were now planted where she had been lying only a moment before. How could any horse be that big, she thought, as she nervously stepped away from him.
'Please don't go, there is no need to be frightened by my great size and strength' said Prince. My breed is known as the Gentle Giants.' So Greta stayed close to him.

Grazing together and talking with him all afternoon, Prince told her that now he was retired he only did occasional light work about the place. Like bringing the trees out of the plantation nearby. He could move safely between the trees on the steep hillside where the tractor could not go, and he would drag logs down to the main trackways.

In his younger days he had lived in the city. He and a friend had worked on the busy streets delivering beer to the public houses. They would take heavy loads of barrels on their dray through the busy streets, stopping at red traffic lights then striding on amongst the buses and cars. He and his friend would wait patiently outside the inns while their drayman heaved and rolled the full barrels, lowering them down to the cellars then lifting the empty ones back up onto the dray.

Prince had enjoyed this work. Passersby would often stop and pat them while they stood patiently waiting, very often feeding from their nosebags which had been carried on a hook under the back of the wagon.

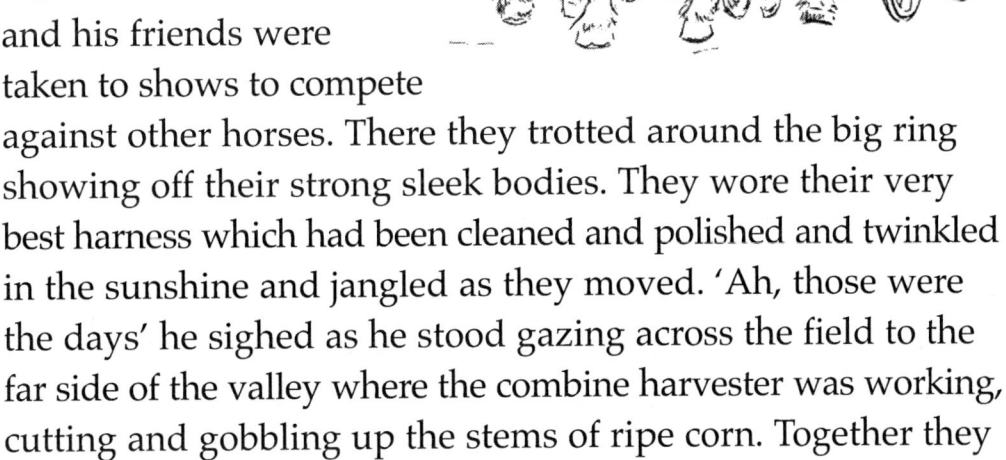

On some special days in the summer he and his friends were taken to shows to compete against other horses. There they trotted around the big ring showing off their strong sleek bodies. They wore their very best harness which had been cleaned and polished and twinkled in the sunshine and jangled as they moved. 'Ah, those were the days' he sighed as he stood gazing across the field to the far side of the valley where the combine harvester was working, cutting and gobbling up the stems of ripe corn. Together they watched as a tractor drawing a trailer moved alongside; a golden stream of grain falling into the trailer before it sped off towards the farm buildings. 'Of course my ancestors used to do all the work on the land, fetching, carrying, hay-making, harvesting, ploughing, rolling and harrowing – all of it, great gangs of us up before dawn to have our feed, then out working in all weathers. It was long hard and heavy work, just as well we had grown so big and strong.

'What do you mean?' asked Greta 'weren't Shire horses always as tall and strong as you are?'

'No, way back in the Middle Ages we were smaller but still enormously strong. We were the Great War horses who carried the Knights into battle. The Knights wore metal amour to protect themselves from the heavy swords, axes and lances with which they fought each other. The armour had little hinged sections at the knees, elbows and fingers so that the knights could move, but it must have felt very awkward. Covered up like that no one would have known who they were and so they wore coloured feathers on their helmets and had their emblems painted onto their shields.'

'The Knights were so weighed down by all the heavy armour that staying in the saddle would have been difficult so, to give them a secure seat to fight from, the saddles had a high pommel in front and a high cantle at the back. To protect us from being wounded in the fighting we too wore armour. The whole lot weighed so much we had to be enormously strong, though not so tall as to be top heavy because we had to be able to gallop into battle.

To be quick and clever at fighting the knights practised at home, making their skills into a sport. They used the Quintain, which was a post set in the ground, it had a swivelling arm at the top. One end had a shield on it at which the knights charged, and tried to strike with their long lances or swords, while the other end had a heavy ball and chain on it. If the rider didn't gallop away quickly enough he would be hit on the back of the head by the ball as the cross-piece swung around.

Jousting was another exercise. Two knights would ride fast towards each other, one on either side of a fence, and try to score a hit or even knock the rider off his horse! Writers and storytellers have told romantic tales of chivalry and jousting which gave which gave much enjoyment to many and although very exciting it was, in fact, horribly dangerous. The sport went out of fashion after the king of France died in a jousting accident. It was about that time that the surviving Great War horses took to hauling and an agricultural way of life, having been bred taller and even stronger to do this work.'

Greta returned to her mother with the imagined clash of arms ringing in her long ears. She wondered if her ancestors had done exciting things and helped humanity in the way that Prince's forefathers had.

THE STORY OF BALAAM

One afternoon Greta was over by the fence next to the stable yard enjoying being petted by the children and watching the ponies and horses being groomed, when a squabble broke out between some of the children, and they called each other names. 'You are useless' shouted one of them, 'you silly ass.'

Greta ran to her mother distressed that the name of her breed should be used as a word of abuse. 'Why should they say that?' Daisy nuzzled her gently, 'let me tell you about a man who called his donkey a silly, useless ass.

Balaam was a famous magician who lived far away and long ago, at a time when the Israelites, who were God's chosen people, were journeying to their Promised Land of Canaan. They came with all their people and great army to the country of Moab, but the king of Moab was frightened of them and did not want them to cross his land because the Israelite army was so large and had fought and won many battles. So the king sent for Balaam to come and curse the Israelites and put a spell upon them. God told Balaam not to go, so he refused. Again the king sent for him, bribing him with offers of riches. This time God told Balaam that he could go, but only to do and say what He told him to. So Balaam saddled his ass and set off, thinking to himself that he would please the king and have the riches, and probably do what God said at the same time.'

God knew what he was thinking and was angry and so he sent one of his angels to stand in the road in front of Balaam to bar his way. When the ass saw the angel standing there with his sword drawn she turned off the road into the field, and Balaam beat her back onto the path shouting at her "you silly ass". A little further on the ass saw the angel again, and this time she tried to squeeze past, but in doing so she crushed her master's foot against the wall and he beat her once more.'

The third time the ass saw the angel was in a very narrow place and so, to avoid him, she lay down under Balaam. He was furious, this time he really set about her with his stick.'

God then allowed the ass to speak and she said, "what have I done wrong? this is the third time you have beaten me?" Balaam was mad at being made a fool of and said "if I had a sword I would kill you here and now."

T he ass answered "am I not still the ass you have ridden all your life and have I ever done anything like this before?" "No" he answered, and with that God opened Balaam's eyes so that he too could see the angel. He bowed down and lay flat on his face in front of the angel who was angry with him for beating his loyal donkey.'

B alaam realised God knew that he had been thinking to cheat him and was ashamed. He travelled on to see the king and even though the king offered Balaam many riches, he did only as God told him.'

'So you see,' Daisy said while Greta stood close to her 'we may appear to be silly asses but God can use us even now, as He used Balaam's ass to teach him to be honest and obedient to God.'

G reta smiled happily to herself as she thought about this story, she was proud to be part of the breed that God had used, as she had felt quite inferior for some days after Shah had told her his tales of the Arabs and of Mohammed.

HIGH TREE LADY - THE THOROUGHBRED'S TALE

Greta spent many long hours that summer in the shade of the great tree, standing beside a chestnut thoroughbred who rested while she lazily swished her tail to keep away the flies. Greta stood so that Lady's tail swept over her head now and again, keeping the flies from her too.

High Tree Lady had been a racehorse, but she had a placid and kindly outlook on life and just had not bothered to gallop as fast as she should have done while racing, and so she had been sold. She was now owned by a young rider who was schooling her ready to compete in three-day events some time soon.

Lady had explained to Greta that it took a lot of concentration and practice to learn the three disciplines of dressage, show jumping and how to gallop bravely across country, jumping the solid and complicated jumps accurately and at speed, putting to the test both the horse and rider. Greta loved to hear Lady explain how she would take shorter strides when coming to one of these jumps and then leap over and out, sometimes landing where the ground was lower than where she had leapt from, and sometimes landing in a lake, sending showers of silvery, watery rainbows high into the air. The crowds around the jump would cheer her as she galloped onwards.

Some of the jumps were frighteningly big, but she and her rider were learning to trust each other. Lady knew that if she did as she was told and tried hard she would be quite safe.

'How do you know what your rider wants you to do and where to go?' asked Greta.

Lady raised her head and made a soft whinny of greeting as she saw her rider coming through the gate by the stable yard.

'If you come and watch through the fence by the schooling paddock I will show you' she said as she and her friend walked away together and disappeared into the stable yard.

The little donkey waited very patiently. She noticed that there was some longer grass with dandelions growing in it just the other side of the fence. If she let her knees sag and put her head on one side she could just reach the juicy stems. The dandelions tasted particularly nice.

Presently Greta saw Lady and her rider come into the schooling area and walk around it several times. Then they trotted in one direction, and then came across the centre to go the other way.

Lady called to Greta 'You see my rider's hands on the reins – I am guided by the gentle but steady feel on my mouth, I bend my head and go whichever way the stronger pressure leads me. My rider's legs urge me forward.

The various degrees of contact of the bit on my mouth, together with the strength of leg pressure tells me what my rider wants me to do.'

Mystified, Greta watched closely. After a while she could plainly see what was happening, how the rider's hands taking a level pressure on the reins brought Lady to a halt and how if she swung her hind-quarters sideways the rider's leg came firmly against her side to hold her straight.

Fascinated, the little donkey watched as her friend went from a good trot into a short, bouncy collected trot and then surged forward with long elegant strides, flicking her toes out in front of her. Then she made lovely turns keeping her legs moving with the same rhythm. 'Some day' sighed Greta, 'when I am older perhaps I too will be able to try doing dressage.'

'Well, I used to do it' said Daisy, who had come to see what her daughter was watching – 'and I was quite good! I even won some rosettes.'

'You did?' Greta looked at her mother in amazement.

'I used to go to shows put to my little carriage. We competed in the driven dressage classes. We did the walking and the different trotting movements quite nicely. I expect when you are older you will learn, and I am sure you will be very good at it too.'

Alone, Greta wandered off thinking about all this and also of nothing in particular, and found herself watching some butterflies as they seemed to dance among the flowers.

RAVEN – THE FELL PONY'S TALE

One hot afternoon while Greta was drinking from the water trough near the gate she saw Raven, a strong black pony, being lead back out to the field.

She had noticed him go off that morning looking his usual sleek and shiny self but now, as he came towards her making for the trough, she saw that he had dry sticky sweat patches on his body in strange places. One streak of sweat going along his sides and one right around him behind his withers, and the front of each shoulder was caked with sweat.

His ears moved back with little twitchy movements as he drank, and she could see that they too had been very wet although now they were dry.

'Ah, that's better' he said. As he lifted his head a thin stream of water ran from his lips back into the trough. 'They usually sponge me down when I have finished, but today they forgot!'

'What have you been doing?' enquired Greta.

'Just a minute , I must have a roll and get rid of some of these tickly patches.' With that, he went a few paces, his legs bending under him until he flopped onto the ground, rubbing his ears into the grass then, with a great heave, he rolled onto his back and over to his other side. He repeated this a few more times before standing up. Letting out a long groan he shook himself, and clouds of hair and dust floated into the air.

He said 'come and graze with me, I am ravenously hungry after my morning's work. I do enjoy working with this group of people, we have such fun it is a real pleasure and privilege.'

'I am glad to hear that, but what have you been doing?' asked Greta.

'I have spent the morning driving in the countryside taking people who cannot walk through the fields and woods. They are disabled, their legs and bodies do not work and behave as other people's do. Some of my friends have to sit in a wheelchair all the time so I am put to a special carriage and their wheelchair is pushed up a ramp at the back of the vehicle. When all is fixed safely they are given the reins and off we drive, just the same as anybody else. I was especially chosen to do this work as I go willingly and trot on nicely for them, and I am steady, reliable and strong.' Then he added 'it is so good that my breed can be useful again, we nearly all died out when there was no more work for us to do.'

'Please tell me what work you did and where you came from?' asked Greta.

'I was born up North, almost as far as Scotland, in the fells and dales of the Pennines. We were small hardy Celtic ponies at the time that the Roman invaders came to Britain and tried to civilise the country. They had a lot of trouble with the Picts, the people from further North, who came South to raid and pilage the land. The Roman Emperor Hadrian planned to build a wall from coast to coast to keep them out. He used the ponies to help with this work, but they were rather small and if he was ever to get this wall built he needed more manpower. He brought workers across the sea from Friesland in the Netherlands and they brought with them their sensible, big, strong black horses. The original Fell and Dales ponies were probably created by breeding the local ponies with these horses.

The ponies continued to live wild on these lonely and lovely hills, learning to thrive on the poor grass that grew there. Farmers used them to work on the land, and they carried the sheep wool from the hill farms down to the mills in the valleys to be spun into cloth. Minerals were mined in these same hills, and they too were carried down to the coast. There were droves of loose ponies walking along the sunken lanes and drove paths across the countryside. They were weighed down with lead and iron-ore weighing 16 stones (102 kg) or more, carried in panniers on their backs. These paths were not surfaced as our roads are today so the ponies didn't need shoes. Strings of pack ponies, with their halter ropes tied to the tail of the pony in front, delivered goods from one side of the country to the other.'

'On dark nights smuggled cargo was brought ashore through the surf on deserted beaches, and loaded silently onto the backs of waiting ponies, the black ponies who trod softly through the night to bring the contraband brandy, tobacco and lace to the inland market towns to be sold in secrecy. Many nights they travelled silently along the lonely lanes, far off the beaten track, avoiding the excise and customs men who were searching them.'

How exciting life must have been in those days thought Greta, but Raven said 'I am glad that I didn't live in those days, some of those ponies trekked 240 miles (386 km) in a week. All that walking must have made them very fit. Some of my cousins still travel along those hill tracks, but now they carry people on trekking holidays.'

Having told her all this he became silent and carried on with the serious matter of grazing.

YORK — THE CLEVELAND BAY'S TALE

There was a big bay horse living in the field to whom Greta had not yet spoken. She watched him now, admiring his thick black mane and tail and his shiny, rich-brown coat which blended to black at his knees and hocks.

This handsome horse whose name was York, was standing in the corner of the field close to the fence, gazing along the road that wound down into the valley and through the village, to the crossroads by the New Cock Inn. Greta followed his gaze and noticed the pub sign with a brightly-painted bird on it swinging slightly in the breeze.

'That picture looks just like the bird that struts and crows in our stable yard' she said.
'Yes, though I wonder if the Inn was named after a bird' he replied, 'even though they have used a picture of a cockerel.'
'What do you mean?' she asked 'what else might it be named for?'
'The olde English word for a hillock is "cocc" and the "hillock" or "cock" horses were probably stabled there. They would be put to a coach or cart to give extra help pulling a heavy load upto the top of the hill.' A lorry growled its way up the hill

sending a cloud of dark evil-smelling fumes drifting towards them, making them both sneeze. Not many lorries used this road now, but cars sped past, hurrying to get to the new motorway that Greta and York could just see in the distance.

'In the olden days, when a heavily-laden coach came along here, it stopped at the Inn and some of the passengers would have to get down to walk up the hill, to ease the load for the horses. Sometimes a "cock" horse or even a pair of them was quickly harnessed and put in front of the team of four horses. The "cock" horse was attached to the coach by a long rope trace that passed between the lead horses and dropped over the end of the pole. Then, with the postillion mounted, the team would start off, perhaps at a gallop, slowing down as the hill became steeper and the coach seemed to get heavier. The horses' feet would slip, sending sparks from their shoes as they fought to get a grip on the flinty road. The coachman would call and cheer encouragement to his flagging team as they hauled the coach safely to the top. Just about here, where we are standing now, they would have stopped to allow the horses to get their breath back. The "cock" horse would have had the trace taken from the pole hook and tucked up across his back and led away to stand on the grass verge while the passengers, who by now had finished their

long walk up the hill, mounted again and the coach would have continued on its way.'

Greta could almost see and smell the sweating horses, their flanks heaving with their laboured breath as her new friend described all this to her. 'The "cock" horse would have walked quietly home to his stable to wait until his help was needed again.' As they stood together they saw the red post van driving through the village. The postman stopped to empty the letter box near the cross roads and then sped off towards the town carrying the letters to the sorting office. York had a faraway look in his eye. 'It never used to be like that' he sighed.

Greta was puzzled 'what wasn't like what?'

'The letters and the post van' he said 'that road in the valley comes from London and along it came all the coaches, carriages and carts. The Mail coach was just one of them. It would have left the main Post Office at St Martins Le Grand in London in the evening. It must have been a wonderful sight to see – all the coaches lined up, each with its splendid team of four horses ready to depart. At 8 o'clock off they went with their red wheels turning and their lamps twinkling out, they travelled through the night and next day to get to their far-off destinations. My breed was developed to be strong and fast with a long stride to cover the many miles that those coaches had to travel. About every 10 miles (16 km) or so the coach stopped at an inn where the next team was ready and waiting. In barely a minute the tired horses were freed from the coach, a fresh team was 'put to' and the coach was on its way again, averaging about 10 miles an hour over the long route. The Post Office employed an armed guard who looked after the letters which were carried in the locker at the rear of the coach. He wore a red livery coat and carried a clock in his satchel to make sure that the coach kept up to time. He also had a long horn on which he blew different tunes to warn people that the coach was coming and to keep the road clear, for it was an offence to slow down the Royal Mail. At some smaller but important villages with a crossroads – perhaps like this one' said York, 'the guard would throw down a bag of letters and pick up another one that was held up high on a cleft stick so he could snatch it as the coach passed by at the gallop.'

Greta imagined the hustle and bustle of that busy road that was now so small and quiet. She stretched her ears hoping to catch the long-past sounds of the horn, the rumble of wheels, the clatter of horses' feet and the chink of the pole chains, bits and harness, but all she could hear was the distant hum of traffic as it rushed along the motorway.

She turned and looked at York. 'Did you ever pull a coach?' she asked.
'Oh yes I was part of a team. We went to all the big shows during the summer months with a coach. We also competed in dressage tests and then went across country making tricky turns through obstacles, I liked that. Best of all was when I sometimes went to help my cousins who work in London and live in grand style at the Royal Mews. They pull carriages on state occasions as well as taking messengers on their daily official rounds.' Deep in thought he paused and drew himself up, arching his neck proudly as he remembered.
'Once when I was staying with them' he said 'I was put with

three of my friends to help them on a state occasion. We went right into the palace courtyard where important personages climbed into the carriages, then we drove along the Mall which was filled with great crowds of cheering people. Flags were waving and the bands were playing, hundreds of cavalry horses trotted along, the sun was glinting on their shiny coats, light was sparkling on the soldiers' armour and lances, it was a bright wonderful noisy pageant. I felt so proud as I pranced along, 'though I remembered my manners and only did a little prancing. I shall always treasure the memory of that day.'

Greta stood with him for a little while longer but he was quiet – lost in his happy memories.

MEGAN – THE WELSH PONY'S TALE

The wind blew rather cold one day and all the horses and ponies gathered in the sheltered part of the field, near the thick hedge where the blackberries grew. Daisy and Greta were amongst them.

Greta noticed that the ponies' coats were looking rather fluffy, not as sleek and shining as they had been a few weeks before. In fact she thought some of her friends looked extremely scruffy, even Megan who usually looked so elegant with her golden-coloured coat and contrasting pale mane and tail. She stood now with her tiny ears pricked forward and a faraway look in her large dark round eyes. Greta went to her and they started to chat about the change in the weather and how the ponies' coats were growing longer and thicker every day now, so that they could be warm and dry through the cold winter months.

Megan said 'we native ponies will have the thickest coats, almost double, with longer hair on top that sheds the wet and leaves the under-coat soft and fluffy, trapping the

warm air against our skin.'
'What are native ponies?' wondered Greta.

So Megan gently and patiently explained to her that after the Ice Age, when the ice had retreated from Britain which was not yet an island, some small wild horses had wandered over from Europe. They made their way to live in different parts of the country where probably the varied food that they found to eat made them grow differently, and they grew to look distinct from each other.

'Mankind lived where it was easier for them to farm the land so the ponies withdrew into the mountainous and wild parts of the islands where the winds roared and the snow settled, where the rain and mists blanked out the landmarks making everything magical and mysterious. Few men came to these remote places so the native ponies grew and flourished.'

'Where are these places' Greta wanted to know, 'and who amongst my friends are descended from these wild ponies?'

'In the North Sea there are rocky islands,' explained Megan 'where the wind blows cold and the grass never grows long and rich as it does in the South. The ponies who live there have learned to thrive by eating this stunted grass and seaweed from the beach. Norse warriors came in their longboats and when they saw how beautiful these Shetland Isles were they decided to stay and fish and farm the land. They used the little ponies that they found there to help them. Over the years these ponies became strong and stocky but remained small whereas their cousins over the water in the highlands and glens of Scotland grew quite a lot bigger.

The Highland ponies or Garrons as they were called, helped the crofters' to farm by doing any kind of work that was required of them, and even now they carry the culled Stags down the mountainsides.

The South West of England, Exmoor, Dartmoor and into Cornwall, and even the Isle of Lundy, was where the moorland ponies thrived. They did not grow as large as the Garrons although they were still tough and sure-footed, with a strong sense of self-preservation which they needed because of the treacherous bogs on these moorlands.Further East along the South coast lived King Rufus, who was very fond of hunting. He preserved the wild woodland and planted more trees and called it the New Forest. Another type of indigenous pony made its home there. The people who lived in the New Forest needed a taller, faster riding animal than the moorland pony so they bred a pony that could gallop faster.

Along the centre of England towards the North is the Pennine range of mountains. The Fell pony's home is on the Western side of the Pennines and the Dales pony orginates from the Eastern side.'

Megan's gaze fell upon a tall grey pony cropping the grass nearby 'and Rafferty, is he a native pony too?' asked Greta.
'Yes my dear, he is from Connemara in the West of Ireland where the grass grows rich. It is said that he gets his good looks from Spain.' Greta looked at Megan enquiringly.
'In the first Elizabethan Age the King of Spain planned to invade England. He embarked his army on a fleet of ships but, during their voyage, a great storm blew up and the armada was scattered. Legend has it that some of the ships were

wrecked on the rocky coast of Connemara and the stallions that were with that great armada swam ashore and joined the herds of wild ponies who lived there.'

' Rafferty is quite an athlete and very sensible. He and his young rider compete with the Pony Club teams in jumping, cross-country and Polo. He is quite good at dressage too. He also carries his rider on a side-saddle, which is the way elegant ladies rode many years ago.'

Megan sighed andshifted her weight, resting her other hind foot, and let her pretty head hang as though she was going to have a little snooze 'that's not all the native breeds' insisted Greta. 'What about you? I have heard that you are Welsh and so is Ivor, though he is far bigger than you are and has all that long hair on the back of his legs which cascades over the top of his feet.'

'Feather' interrupted Megan, 'that hair is known as feather. You should see him when he trots out, stepping high, bending his knees and stretching forward – he looks magnificent, especially when he is put to his trade van at a show. He used to work in London with his old owner. They had a London trolley and with it they collected old iron and rags, anything that was not wanted anymore and that his governor could sell for cash. As they went along the streets the old man shouted out 'Rag an' bone – any old iron' and rang his hand-bell to let people in the houses know that he was there and to bring things out. They also carried vegetables, fruit and flowers from the market to the little shop run by his 'missus'. Sometimes they built up a wonderful display of produce on the trolley and sold it from there.

When the old folks retired from business they gave Ivor to their grandson, that's why he came to live here with us. The grandson is a butcher and owns a very smart van that in the olden days was used with a horse to deliver meat to customers' houses. The van is cunningly designed with slatted panels in the front so, when the horse trots fast, a draught of air blows over the meat keeping it cool and fresh even on the hottest of summer days.'

Greta looked across at the short-backed cob with his rich bay coat, his full mane and tail had a lovely wave in it. His four white stockings were a little muddy just now, but she had seen him one day when they were dazzlingly clean as he was standing in the yard waiting to go to a show.

Megan continued, 'he also has a nice example of a round-back gig which he uses in the private driving classes and for rallies when he enjoys driving out with others along country lanes where they stop for picnics, or at a pub for some refreshment.'

'This is all most interesting, but I would so much like to know about you as well' said Greta.

'Ivor is a Welsh Cob and I am a Welsh Mountain pony,' said Megan. 'My ancestors roamed the Welsh mountains, our origins go so far back they are lost in the mists of time. For generations we have been valued for our elegance and stamina. We have played an important role in the history of

commerce as driving ponies, but we take greatest pride in being a perfect riding pony. We are not too broad in the back, which means we are comfortable for children and there is a height to suit everyone, but we are active and jump well.

'Our kindness and generosity gives children confidence. We are strong and can carry adults. I loved teaching my little owner we had such fun together, at first on a rein with Mother or Father leading me. We would walk for miles and sometimes even go to a show. Later I was led from a horse which one of them rode.

We went hacking out along bridle-paths, over the downs and through woods. When my young rider was proficient enough we went out by ourselves and sometimes met other children on their ponies.

We went to Pony Club rallies and camps where we learned so much, and competed at gymkhanas where I was particularly clever at the bending race, curving my body from one side to the other around the poles. If my young rider remembered to keep the toes tucked in we nearly always won. I was very fast, being not too tall so my young rider could vault onto my back at a gallop.'

We went to the Horse of the Year Show with the Pony Club team and raced in the arena under the floodlights.

I shall never forget the cheering of the crowd and all the excitement of that week.'

When my young rider grew too tall for me I was sent away on loan to another family who had two children. I taught them both, they were kind and we had fun but I always missed my own rider. When these children grew too big for me I was so pleased to come back home.

I learned to go in a nice little carriage in which Mother and Father used to drive me. At the weekends we would go out with others, sometimes stopping to have a picnic.

My young rider occasionally came with us but preferred to ride the bigger ponies. I was a bit sad although I always knew that I was still special.'

'I have become old and stiff and don't do much nowadays, but I am proud of having started my young rider off so well. It is my young rider, now grown up, that you can see schooling in the sand arena riding your friend High Tree Lady.'

A WINTER'S TALE

The weather was cold now and the horses and ponies were taken into the stables at night, which left Daisy and Greta alone in the big field. They spent their nights in the field shelter where a net of hay was tied up for them each evening.

On very wet days the ponies did not come out to the field at all, and the donkeys just stood in the cosy shelter and watched the rain making huge puddles that joined together until the water lay in a great sheet over part of the field.

The donkeys could see the sand manége behind the stables and when the rain stopped the ponies were brought out for exercise, either driven on long reins or trotting and cantering in a circle round their owners who controlled them by a lunge line. Greta watched with great interest. She saw that some of her friends had been clipped and where the hair was short the colour had changed.

She hardly recognised Shah whose legs and the top of his back were bright chestnut and the rest of him was a pale yellowy pink colour.

At weekends and half term the ponies were ridden in the manége, some concentrating on their dressage and others practising their jumping. Greta missed the company of the others and with only her mother to talk to she was getting bored and for something to do she started to gnaw the wood of the shelter, which made Daisy rather cross.

One day when the sun was shining and the wind had dried the puddles up a little, Ivor was turned out with them for just a short while. He told her of the streets crowded with people rushing around with big bags of "things". He had seen this when he had gone with his carriage into the nearby town centre carrying a jolly man with a long red coat and white beard whose name was Father Christmas. He had a sack from which he gave toys to a lot of noisy children who had come especially to see him. Ivor said 'in the town there are many fir trees decorated with shiny balls and twinkling lights. The people seemed to be very happy and the sound of music was everywhere.'

Greta asked after Hamish but Ivor had not seen him since he had been taken away in a horsebox some days ago. She thought longingly of him and his friends who were working at the theatre in the pantomime Cinderella.

How she wished she could see these things instead of staying in the boring old field. Why should everyone else have interesting things happen to them – she felt very left out.

Then something amazing happened!

One morning the children came. They sloshed laughing and squealing through the mud. Their wellies became stuck and they nearly stepped out of them, leaving them behind.

They brought head collars with them and some delicious burnt toast.

The donkeys were led into the stable yard where they were tied up and given a thorough groom. Greta had a very long and woolly coat with a lot of dried mud in it. Daisy's coat was not quite so long but just as muddy.

The children huffed and puffed as they brushed until the donkeys looked clean and their coats felt soft. When all this grooming was finished they were shut up in a stable and the children went home.

'Well this is a bit different,' said Greta finishing off the last crusts of toast, 'what next?'

'I think' replied her mother 'that we are both going to be in a Nativity play.'

'A play? How exciting, what is it all about? Will I be the main attraction?'

'The main attraction is the story. Everyone in it is important. Just be on your best behaviour, stay close to me, watch and listen and you will discover what it is all about.'

The night was cold and clear. As they walked into the village they saw crowds of people gathering on the far side of the green outside The Star Inn. Greta could hear music and the sound of singing. She could see lights shining onto the Inn and beside it an open-fronted garage which looked almost like a stable. She stood close to her mother remembering what she had been told.

A lady called Mary, who was wearing a long blue dress and cape, was helped up onto Daisy's back and a young man with a pretend beard stuck on his chin – his name was Joseph – took the headcollar rope and they all set off together towards the Inn.

When they got there the crowd was so big there was no room for Mary and Joseph to go inside, so instead the landlord showed them to the stable, where Mary dismounted and Daisy was tied up.

Ahush came over the crowd and they listened as a young boy sang all by himself a beautiful song that told the story of the first Christmas when – "Once, in Royal David's city, stood a lowly cattle shed, where a mother laid her baby in a manger for his bed. Mary was that mother mild, Jesus Christ her little child".

Greta looked into the manger where everyone else was looking and there, lying on the hay, was a baby!

The crowd started singing again and she listened to the words. They sang about shepherds in a field taking care of their sheep when an angel suddenly appeared. He told them not to be afraid, that he had brought them and all the people everywhere wonderful news about the baby's birth and told them they should go and see Him, giving them directions to where He was to be found. Presently Greta saw a boy and four men coming along, they had with them a big lamb that walked quietly on a lead, they came and smiled at the baby and then sat down nearby.

There was more singing, this time about kings following a star that "went before them", and how it had stopped and shone over the stable. With this there was a clattering of hooves and three gentlemen from the Orient arrived on horses. They wore splendid robes with crowns on their heads and brought with them presents, which they gave to Mary for her baby.

The crowd fell silent again and listened while someone spoke. The speaker finished by wishing everybody a happy Christmas and inviting the faithful people to sing again one last triumphant hymn. This was so loud and happy that Greta joined in the singing, her hawing was louder than the trumpets.

'Allelujah'

Now that the play was over, children came to stroke and pat the donkeys, ruffling their furry coats with cold little fingers, feeding them apples and sweets, it was hard to tell who enjoyed themselves most, the pleased parents, or excited children, or two very happy donkeys.

Back home again in the field shelter Greta and Daisy ate their hay and talked about the evening.

'What happened to the baby in the story?' Greta asked her mother.

'You remember the three wise men that had followed the star? they didn't know where to find the baby so they visited King Herod to ask him, but he didn't know either. He commanded them to come back when they had found the baby that was born to be King, so that he too could visit. They went and found the baby and gave his mother the gifts that they had brought for him, which were gold, the sweetly-scented resins named frankincense and myrrh.

Now, after they had seen the baby, these wise men had a dream that it was important that they should go home by another route and not return to the King. When jealous King Herod found this out he was furious, and sent his soldiers to kill all boy babies in the area. But our little family had escaped in the night, helped of course by their donkey.

The baby grew up into a wonderful man called Jesus, who cared about all people everywhere and, I expect, about donkeys too. He was the King of Kings, and when he decided to return to the c ity of Jerusalem he sent his friends out to find a donkey for him to ride. They found a young unridden donkey whose owner seemed to be expecting them and was delighted to lend him to Jesus. The crowds had thrown down palm leaves along the streets as a sign of welcome and cheered as he rode past.

So once again we were able to serve Jesus, God's Son. The sign of a cross became his emblem and we have that mark upon our backs.'

Greta stopped pulling the hay from her net and wondered about the baby who grew to be a man and whose ideas still help to guide people all these many centuries later. She left the cosy shed and stepped outside into the sparkling cold night. She looked up into the dark sky set with millions of twinkling stars and thought about the first Christmas.

She fancied that there was one star that was bigger and brighter than all the rest. She felt as though she was brimming over with happiness and love.

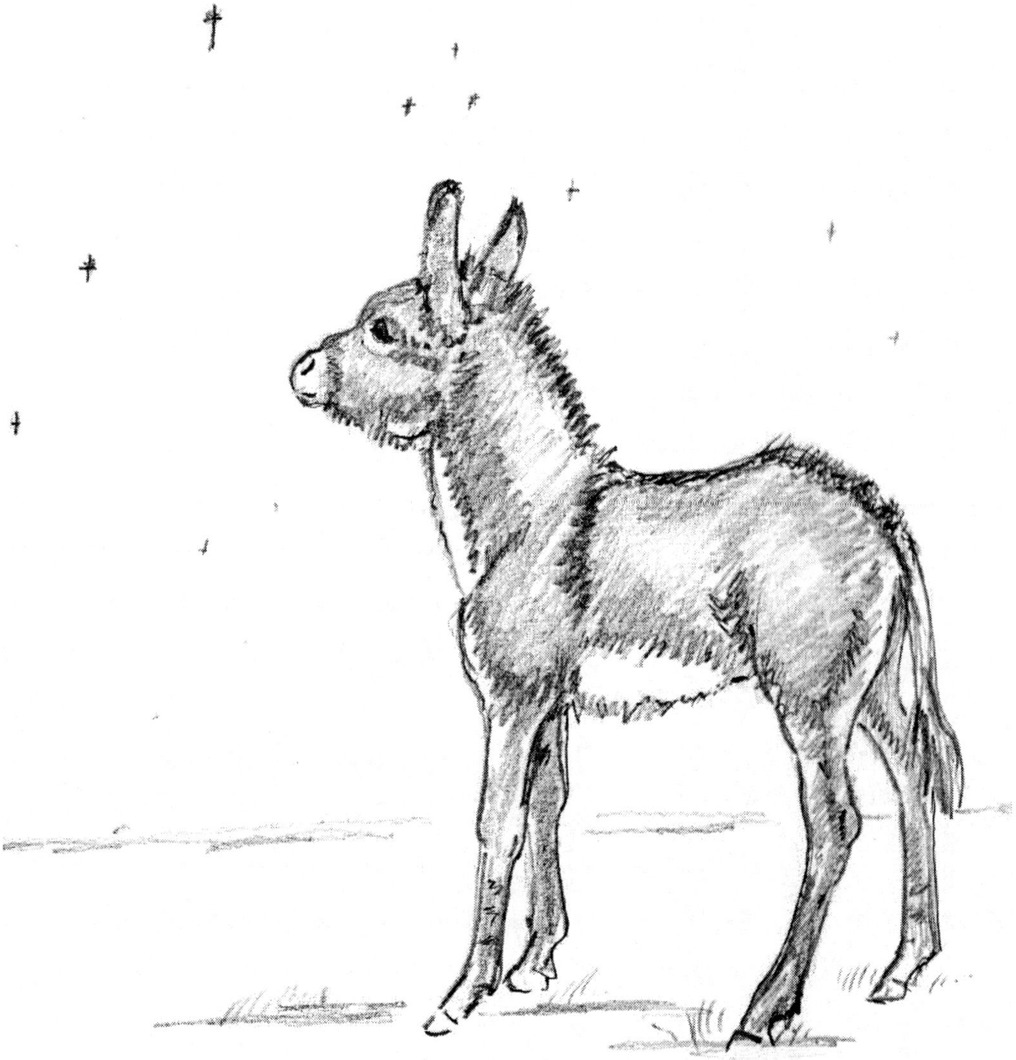

Arab Horse Society
01672 521411
www.arabhorsesociety.org

British Carraige Dogs Society
www.carriagedog.org

British Connemara Pony Society
01289 388800
www.britishconnemaras.co.uk

British Dalmation Club
01543 490849
www.britishdalmationclub.org.uk

British Driving Society
01473 892001
www.britishdrivingsociety.co.uk

British Horse Society
08701 202244
www.bhs.org.uk

Cleveland Bay Horse Society
01904 489731
www.clevelandbay.com

Dales Pony Society
01629 640439
www.dalespony.org

Dartmoor Pony Society
01269 844303
www.dartmoorponysociety.com

Donkey Breed Society
01732 864414
www.donkeybreedsociety.co.uk

Endurance GB
02476 698863
www.endurancegb.co.uk

Exmoor Pony Society
01884 839930
www.exmoorponysociety.org.uk

Fell Pony Society
01768 353100
www.fellponysociety.org

Highland Pony Society
01738 451861
www.highlandponysociety.com

New Forest Pony Breeding & Cattle Society
01425 672775
www.newforestpony.com

The Pony Club
0247 6698300
www.pcuk.org

Riding for the Disabled Association
0845 6581082
www.rda.org.uk

Shetland Pony Stud Book Society
01738 623471
www.shetlandponystudbooksociety.co.uk

Shire Horse Society
01733 234451
www.shire-horse.org.uk

Welsh Pony & Cob Society
01970 617501
www.wpcs.uk.com

Working Horse Trust
01892 750105
www.theworkinghorsetrust.org

ISBN 142512185-3